Bodine

The PRINTER'S APPRENTICE

Also by Stephen Krensky

The Iron Dragon Never Sleeps

The PRINTER'S APPRENTICE

Stephen Krensky

Illustrated by Madeline Sorel

DELACORTE PRESS

Published by Delacorte Press
Bantam Doubleday Dell Publishing Group, Inc.
1540 Broadway
New York, New York 10036

Library of Congress Cataloging-in-Publication Data
Krensky, Stephen.
The printer's apprentice / Stephen Krensky; illustrated by
Madeline Sorel.
p.   cm.
Summary: In 1735 in New York City, a young printer's apprentice
learns about the importance of freedom of speech when the printer
Peter Zenger is arrested and tried for writing articles criticizing the
government.
ISBN 0-385-32095-7
1. New York (N.Y.)—History—Colonial period. ca. 1600–1775—
Juvenile fiction.   2. Zenger, John Peter, 1697–1746—Fiction.
[1. New York (N.Y.)—History—Colonial period, ca. 1600–1775—
Fiction.   2. Apprentices—Fiction.   3. Freedom of speech—Fiction.
4. Newspapers—Fiction.]   I. Sorel, Madeline, ill.   II. Title.
PZ7.K883Pr   1995
[Fic]—dc20   94-36721
                                                         CIP
                                                          AC
The text of this book is set in 14-point Adobe Caslon.
Book design by Susan Clark
Manufactured in the United States of America
June 1995
10   9   8   7   6   5   4   3   2   1

For my father-in-law,
Rudy Frongello

☛ ONE

Gus Croft was waiting.

He stood silently on the New York waterfront. All around him sailors were rigging sails or checking their fishing gear. Others were moving goods to and from ships in the harbor.

Gus wiped his brow. It was hot for late September. Across the East River, Gus could see the trees of Brooklyn stirring in a slight breeze. *Breuckelen,* the Dutch had called it when they had settled New York over a hundred years earlier. Of course, they had also called New York by another name—*Nieuw Amsterdam.*

I

Gus was watching a dinghy approach from H.M.S. *Hesperus*. It was carrying a packet of letters from London. His master, William Bradford, printed the *New York Gazette,* a four-page weekly newspaper that always included the latest news from England. The news in the letters would be fresh—just a few weeks old.

Gus had been an apprentice for a year. After his ninth birthday and his father's death from smallpox, his mother had brought him to work for Master Bradford.

Most tradesmen—whether printers, silversmiths, mechanics, or tanners—had apprentices. In all seasons they worked six days a week from early morning until night. The boys were paid no wages, but over time they learned a trade.

A few minutes later the second mate from the *Hesperus* climbed out of the boat. He knew Gus from other voyages.

"Off you go!" he said, tossing Gus a packet of letters and a small package.

"Thank you," said Gus. He turned and headed back down the pier.

"You there! Boy!"

Two sailors were hailing Gus. They both staggered a little as they walked, as sailors often did when they had been long at sea.

"My name's Flint," said the bigger one, smiling to reveal a few missing teeth. "What's your business here?"

Gus straightened up. "I picked up some mail from the *Hesperus*. There was some delay—the winds or the tides, I think."

"The winds or the tides?" Flint snorted. "What say you to that, Mr. Hyde?"

The other sailor spat into the water. "I'd say he hadn't left much out. But I reckon we could learn him quick enough. Ever been to sea, boy?"

"Once," said Gus. He and his parents had come to New York from England three years before. Gus had few pleasant memories of the voyage. He had spent most of his time seasick below deck.

The sailors eyed Gus closely. He was lean as a beanpole, and his ink-stained shirt and coat did nothing to fill him out. Still, he looked healthy enough, if a bit pale. After a few weeks at sea the paleness would burn off.

"Our captain's looking for a new cabin boy. The last one fell off the mast during a storm."

"I already have a master," said Gus. "I'm a printer's apprentice."

Flint and Mr. Hyde moved slightly apart, blocking Gus's path. "An educated cabin boy," said Mr. Hyde. "The captain will be pleased."

He lunged at Gus, but misjudged a little, and Gus ducked under his arm. Flint tried to grab him, but Gus twisted out of his grasp. Then they both lost their balance. Gus fell to the pier.

Flint toppled into the water.

Mr. Hyde laughed harshly. "You're a slippery eel, aren't you, boy?"

He would have grabbed Gus then, but a cry from the water distracted him.

"Mr. Hyde, help me! I can't swim!"

Gus had heard tales of sailors who had never learned to swim, but he had always thought them fanciful.

Mr. Hyde hesitated—and Gus scampered away out of reach. The last thing he heard was Mr. Hyde, as he threw a line into the water. "The captain will not be pleased, Flint," he said. "Not pleased at all."

Gus didn't stop running until he passed the King's Arms, a popular tavern at the corner of

Nassau and Fulton streets. There he almost collided with someone coming the other way.

"Whoa, there!"

A large hand grabbed Gus by the shoulder. It was attached to an equally large arm and body.

"Oh, it's you, Gus," said Zach. He was a lawyer's apprentice who lived around the corner from the Bradfords. Zachariah Bennett was a farmer's son, and built like an ox, but he had a head for book learning. So his father had apprenticed him to a lawyer in town.

"What's your hurry?" asked Zach. "Remember, 'Haste makes waste.' "

Zach was always quoting from *Poor Richard's Almanack*. The almanac, published each year in Philadelphia, contained a calendar and articles on different subjects. The author was Richard Saunders and the printer was B. Franklin. Gus didn't know if Mr. Saunders was real. Writers often used invented names to keep their real identities secret.

Gus took a deep breath. "In this case I think even Poor Richard would approve," he said. "You would not believe what just happened to me."

He told Zach about the sailors.

Zach nodded soberly. "I've heard of such things. There's no use trying to get justice done. Their ship will be gone on the evening tide. It may not return to New York for years." He sighed. "It is troubling that such actions go on. This is 1734, after all, not the Dark Ages."

"True enough," said Gus. "But if I don't hurry, it will be 1735 before I return to the shop. Good day to you, Zach."

And off he went before Zach or Poor Richard could think of a reply.

☞ TWO

William Bradford's printing shop was on Pearl Street. It took up the whole ground floor with the main press toward the back. Nearby was the compositing bench and a long table for making up forms.

When Gus walked in, Master Bradford was standing at a desk, closely examining a copper mold. It was filled with all the letters and punctuation marks of a handbill. Now Master Bradford was checking it for mistakes.

"You're late," said the master, running a hand through his wispy hair.

Gus knew better than to make excuses, even ones involving sailors and kidnapping. Life was full of excuses, Master Bradford had often commented. It was best to ignore them and get on about your business.

"I'm sorry, Master Bradford."

"Sorry doesn't set the type. Sorry doesn't clean the presses."

"No, master."

"If you wish to continue in my service, you will do well to remember this."

Gus nodded. Master Bradford never raised his voice when he was angry, but somehow this made his anger all the more terrible.

"Do you wish to see the packet?" Gus asked meekly.

"Shortly," said Master Bradford without looking up. "First I must finish this for the governor."

Gus nodded. The master was a marvel—over seventy years old and still as active as ever. He printed books and broadsides, pamphlets and official notices. His most regular work was for the government, especially Governor Cosby.

A handwritten copy of the handbill sat on the nearby table. Gus read it to himself.

Strike me blue! thought Gus. The governor was offering a reward of £20 for anyone identifying the author of the "Scandalous Songs or Ballads, highly defaming the Administration of His Majesty's government in this province." The words had been published in the *New-York Weekly Journal,* New York's other weekly newspaper. The author, however, had not used his real name.

Gus wasn't sure what *scandalous* and *defaming* meant, but he could tell the governor was angry. Twenty pounds was a lot of money. Why, a person could live for months and months on such a fortune.

"Gathering cobwebs, Gus?" remarked Master Bradford. He always said that when an apprentice had stood in one place too long.

Gus got busy sorting some used type into the proper cases. Capital letters went into the upper case. The others went into the lower case. In each case, the most commonly used letters were grouped in the middle. Rarely used letters, like *q*, *x*, and *z*, were put in the bottom left corner.

"I remember young Zenger gathering cobwebs," the master muttered. "He seems to have overcome the habit."

Gus knew the story of Peter Zenger. He had come to New York from Bavaria in 1710. At thirteen he had become Master Bradford's apprentice.

The young Peter had lived with Bradford's family for eight years. He had eaten with them and worn their clothes. He had received any rewards or punishments the Bradfords chose to give him.

After some time away Zenger had returned to set up his own shop in New York. Some months ago a group of the governor's foes had helped him start another newspaper.

"The governor has been trying to get Zenger arrested for months," said Master Bradford. "This latest outrage may do it."

"I hope so, sir."

"You would do best to stay clear of politics, Gus. In such a hornet's nest it is easy to get stung."

Gus nodded. Almost every article Zenger published was critical of the government. Why, last December, Zenger had even made fun of the high sheriff. In an advertisement the sheriff had been compared to "a monkey of the larger sort."

It was no secret, though, that the governor was unpopular. He was not elected, like the members of the New York Assembly. He was the appointed representative of the King of England.

"Done," said the master, rubbing his eyes. He stretched his arms over his head.

"Let's see what you brought, Gus."

He opened a letter and began to read.

"The war in Poland goes on. France is on one side, Austria and Russia on the other. . . . A composer named Bach has written something new." He stroked his chin. "Not much there, really. What's in here, I wonder."

He opened the small package.

"Why, look at these. They're from a friend in London."

He held up a short, thin wooden stick.

"What is it?" asked Gus.

Master Bradford consulted his letter. "It's a

new kind of writing instrument. A pencil. My friend claims they will be very popular."

"A pencil?" Gus repeated. What a funny name it was.

"Whittle me a point on it," said the master. "Then we'll try it out."

They both turned as the shop door opened. A well-dressed figure walked in. His ample stomach was hidden beneath a velvet waistcoat with silver buttons.

"Good day to you, Squire," said Master Bradford. He wiped his hands on his long leather apron.

Squire Eustace Wilson was a rich lawyer and friend of the governor. He was also a nervous man, one who turned suddenly at the slightest noise. Whenever he did so, the powder in his wig jumped off in a little cloud.

The squire tapped his walking stick sharply on the floor. "Good day, Master Bradford. The governor asked me to check how his handbill is coming."

"It will be ready tomorrow," said Master Bradford. "I was just reviewing the text."

"That is good. The *Weekly Journal* must be

stopped! The governor is furious at this attack on his dignity, this assault on his character. He will not condone this breach of public decorum."

"Huzzah!" Gus almost shouted. The squire certainly had a way with words. Poor Peter Zenger. He was in for it now.

The squire paused for breath. "Is that understood?"

"Completely," Master Bradford said evenly.

One thing was certain, thought Gus. The governor had no intention of letting Zenger make a monkey out of him.

☞ THREE

The next month passed quickly for Gus. Every day there was a press to clean and type to set. The hours were long and ink-stained, and his fingers were constantly nicked with paper cuts.

Learning how to run a press was important, but, as Master Bradford explained, there was more to being a printer than that.

"Ink and paper do not grow in gardens," the master was fond of saying. "You must learn to make your own."

Ink was something Gus knew about. It was

made from flaxseed oil and a fine soot called lampblack. All colonial printers made their own. It was a smelly, messy job, but not really difficult.

Paper was another matter. "Do you not get your paper from the mill in New Jersey?" Gus had asked.

"True enough," said Master Bradford. "But it is the only paper mill between Philadelphia and Boston. What if it closed? Or there was a fire?"

Gus didn't know.

"Besides," said Master Bradford, "paper is a great expense. It can cost as much as twelve shillings a ream."

Gus blinked. He could eat for a week on twelve shillings.

"And a ream's only five hundred pages. A printer uses hundreds of reams in a year. Can you imagine the sums involved? I thought not. Therefore you must learn to make your own paper."

As Gus had soon discovered, papermaking was a lengthy process. It began with clothing rags, white linen if possible. If the rags were not white to begin with, they were bleached with lye

in a big kettle. Then the rags were thrown into a Hollander, a machine that shredded them into pulp.

The soupy pulp was put into a vat. From there it was scooped up into a papermaking mold, a wood frame crisscrossed with thick and thin wires. Gus had done this poorly at first. It took practice to learn how much pulp to scoop up, how to drain the water from it, and when to drop the thin layer of pulp onto a felt pad.

When Gus finally had made a pile of new sheets, he placed them beneath a press and carefully squeezed out the water from them. Then he laid the sheets out to dry.

The first paper Gus had made was thick and lumpy. Master Bradford had just shaken his head at it. With practice the sheets became thinner and flatter, good enough to use.

Making paper required more rags than Master Bradford's household could supply. One source for additional ones was the grand home of the Van Winkles, where his mother was the family cook. Gus stopped there on Mondays when he delivered the *Gazette*.

The Van Winkle house was near the Collect Pond. Like many Dutch homes, it had a stoop before the door. There the Van Winkle family sat on benches in the evening and visited with friends passing by.

Gus found his mother in the garden inspecting pumpkins and squash. Mistress Croft was a large and dedicated cook. She never sent a dish to the family table without knowing what it tasted like first.

"I've got my eye on you," she was saying, wagging her finger at a large pumpkin. "You'll make a lovely pie in another fortnight."

"Good day, Mother," said Gus.

"Augustus! Come sit down. You look hungry. I've saved you some bread and cheese."

While Gus ate, his mother read the newspaper. She inspected the *Gazette* carefully, holding it with the tips of her fingers. It was the Van Winkles' subscription, and she did not wish to crease the pages.

"I have told you before, Mother. Master Bradford wishes you to have your own copy."

"That's generous of him, Augustus. But that

would leave you one copy short. I don't want the Bradford printing establishment ruined because of me."

"Mother, Master Bradford is a very successful man. We print five hundred copies of the *Gazette* every week. I don't think one more—"

"Fortunes have turned on less chance than that," his mother declared. She rattled the newspaper. "I see Governor Cosby is making more proclamations. That strutting peacock only wants to get rich."

"Mother!"

"Well, it's true. First, he tried to do old Mayor Van Dam out of his salary. And now he spends his time thinking up new ways to make his fortune. Not that I'll read about it in the *Gazette!*"

Gus frowned. "Where do you read about it, Mother?"

"In the *Weekly Journal,* naturally."

"Mother, you shouldn't read that! It's our competition."

"Maybe so, but Peter Zenger has a point of view worth knowing about. Anyway, I have no more time to talk now, Augustus. The family has cousins coming over for supper. I have much to prepare." She shook her head. "There's a sleepy nephew with straw between his ears and a stomach that knows no bottom." She smiled. "As it happens, young Rip likes my cooking."

Gus stood up to leave.

"I'll see you on Sunday, then. But, please, Mother, if you must read the *Weekly Journal* . . ."

"Yes?"

"Could you do it when no one is looking?"

Mistress Croft smiled at him. "I'll try, Augustus, I'll try."

☞ FOUR

On the first Sunday in November, Gus and Zach were sitting near the Collect Pond. It was the anniversary of the day they had first met.

The meeting had occurred soon after Gus had arrived in New York. A group of boys were taunting him about his clothes. There was some pushing and shoving—and there might have been more—when Zach arrived. He was not yet a lawyer's apprentice, only a farmer's son in town for market day.

"You didn't know your way around then," Gus said, remembering.

"True," said Zach. "But I knew an unfair fight when I saw one. That's why I took your side."

"You looked like an overgrown rainbarrel," said Gus.

Zach shrugged. "It was a good look, wasn't it? None of the boys wanted to fight me. They just slunk off muttering about having their fun spoiled."

From that day on, Zach and Gus had been friends. And when Gus later discovered that Zach wanted to learn to read, he offered to teach him. This was a great gift, for neither of Zach's parents knew their letters. Without that skill, he could never have become a lawyer's apprentice.

"What are your plans for Tuesday?" Zach asked.

Tuesday, November 5th, was Guy Fawkes Day. Guy Fawkes had been a conspirator in the Gunpowder Plot, an unsuccessful plan to blow up London's Parliament buildings in 1605.

Every year since then the day had been celebrated. Actually it was the night that Gus enjoyed most. That was when people paraded through the streets in strange costumes and played pranks on their neighbors.

"I want to be a pirate," said Gus. "Like Captain Kidd."

Zach brushed a leaf from his hair. "William Kidd was no pirate."

Gus was surprised. "That's what I've always heard," he said.

"It was just a lie his enemies spread," said Zach. "My grandfather knew Kidd. He told me what happened. Forty years ago the governor here set up Captain Kidd with a ship and crew. They were supposed to hunt for pirates off the coast of Africa. The governor and his friends were hoping that Kidd would capture a lot of pirate ships and treasure. As backers of his voyage, they would get their share of the plunder."

"So what happened?"

"Kidd never made the captures they expected. The governor and his friends were so disappointed they accused him of turning pirate himself. It was the best way to explain their losses. Kidd was captured, sent to London, and hanged. My grandfather always said the rope had found the wrong neck to stretch."

"Well, we could still be pirates," said

Gus. "The pirates Captain Kidd was sent to catch."

Zach had no objection to that.

Two nights later they met at the corner of Broad and Beaver streets. Gus had traded his leather apron for a ragged waistcoat. He had also darkened his face with ashes and hung a black patch over one eye.

Zach was dressed much the same. He carried a stout quarterstaff and wore an enormous cape. Some colorful rags were sewn in a ball on the cape's right shoulder.

"What's that?" Gus asked.

Zach patted his ball of rags. "A parrot, of course."

Gus laughed. "Kind of a sickly parrot."

"He might be a little tired," Zach admitted. "Being a pirate's parrot is hard work."

"I meant no insult," said Gus, smiling. "Shall we go?"

In Hanover Square they met others dressed up as well. Everyone then marched through the streets, whooping and hollering to wake the dead.

The crowd broke up at last. The older members headed for the taverns to quench their thirst. The younger members headed home.

Gus and Zach whistled their way down Broad Street. Dim lights were visible behind the curtained windows. In one, though, the lanterns still burned brightly.

"Who is working at such a late hour?" asked Gus.

"That's Peter Zenger's shop," said Zach. "He has lately moved from Smith Street."

Gus peered in the window. Zenger's press was older than Master Bradford's, and the few tables and chairs did not match. Still the shop was neat and well organized. But was this not to be expected? After all, Master Bradford had taught Zenger well.

"What's he doing?" Zach asked.

"Setting type," said Gus.

Zenger was picking out the letters he needed from the cases. These letters he used to create words in a line on a compositor's stick. The printer worked quickly. His eyes never left the handwritten copy, but his hands knew just where to find each letter in the cases.

When the compositor's stick was full, Zenger spaced the words with blanks to make the whole line the proper length.

"Zenger is a hard worker," said Zach.

Gus snorted. "Maybe so, but he makes mistakes. Why, a year ago, the first issue of his newspaper was dated October fifth, though the true date was November fifth."

"I know Zenger's English is not perfect," said Zach. "German is his first language. Still, he labors long hours for his customers. As Poor Richard says, 'The used key is always bright.'"

"Well," said Gus, "this *key* has a companion."

Gus was right. Zenger was not alone. Another man was standing at a desk in the back. He was busily writing on some foolscap paper.

"That's James Alexander," said Zach. "He writes much of the copy for the newspaper. But he is a lawyer, too. And a brave man. He fought in Scotland with the rebels in 1715. He is still fighting men who misuse their power."

"You speak rashly," said Gus. "The governor is a royal appointee. To question him is like questioning the king himself."

"The king does not make every decision that goes out under his name," said Zach.

Gus had never thought much about what the king did or didn't do.

The clip of a staff on the cobblestone street interrupted his thoughts.

"The rattle-watch is coming," he whispered.

Zach nodded. The watchman, called a rattle-watch, made regular rounds through the town. He carried a lantern and a large rattle or klopper that he struck to frighten away thieves.

The rattle-watch stopped.

"Eleven o'clock and all's well!" he called out.

Gus and Zach pulled back into the shadows as the rattle-watch passed. Then Zach motioned for Gus to follow him.

Neither of them made a sound on foot, but Zach began to strike his staff on the buildings in time with the rattle-watch's steps.

The rattle-watch stopped.

Gus and Zach froze.

The rattle-watch started up again, and Zach resumed his tapping.

The rattle-watch turned around.

"Who's there?" he called out.

Gus smothered a laugh.

"I don't take kindly to mischief-makers," warned the rattle-watch. "Follow me at your peril. You will not like getting a taste of my klopper."

"He's right about that," Zach whispered.

"Come on," said Gus. "I have an idea. I know where he stops next on the hour. He always chooses the same place."

They turned down a side street and circled ahead of the rattle-watch. Gus halted in front of a lantern in Hanover Square. There were lanterns lit in front of every seventh house. Beside this one there was also a rainbarrel. Near it was a watering can.

"The Browns live here," Gus explained. "They are dedicated gardeners—and they have a second-floor balcony overlooking the street."

He half-filled the watering can from the rainbarrel and started climbing a sturdy trellis at the side of the house. Zach followed.

They reached the balcony and waited excitedly until the rattle-watch approached. The distinc-

tive *clip-clop* of his steps echoed around the silent houses.

He came to a stop at the lantern directly beneath Gus and Zach.

"Past midnight and all's well!"

"Now," whispered Gus.

Zach tilted the watering can over, sprinkling the rattle-watch with its contents. Then he fell back.

The rattle-watch looked up in surprise. The sky was clear. He held his lantern aloft, but saw only shadows.

"Chance of rain, perhaps," wailed the rattle-watch, and continued on his rounds.

☞ FIVE

Some days the raw November air crept into every corner of Master Bradford's shop. Gus was constantly rubbing his fingers and finding reasons to pass by the fire.

One morning his numb fingers betrayed him. He dropped a completed form on the floor. It was reduced to pie—a jumble of type that took him all morning to set right.

The weather affected Master Bradford as much as anyone. He became impatient at any delays. He was especially gruff when missing a sort—a letter in the particular type style he was using—while setting type. Being out of sorts often ruined his mood for hours.

There were other pressures as well. Bradford had fathered two sons and a daughter by his first wife, who had died in 1731. He had since married again. His new wife had been a widow with several grown children of her own. Gus had often seen them come to his master for money.

After one such visit Master Bradford called Gus to his side.

"I have an errand for you, my boy," he said. "I had planned to do it myself, but I have wasted too much of the day already." He handed Gus a leather satchel. "The governor asked me to print a special notice. I want you to bring him a draft for his approval. Make sure you give it to the governor himself. I don't want to risk it getting lost or mislaid."

Although it was only the middle of the week, Gus took a moment to wash up. Then he put on a fresh shirt and pushed his hair out of his face. The governor would not appreciate a dirty messenger.

It was cold outside. The poor weather had driven away the chickens and pigeons that usually cluttered the streets. A few pigs, though, were still rooting about for scraps.

Gus was nervous as he walked. He always defended the governor—to his mother and Zach—but he knew the stories about him. The governor's enemies said he was quick-tempered, jealous, and greedy. They faulted him for raising money by selling government appointments.

Gus soon reached the governor's home at Fort George. Although not as grand as some private houses, the governor's quarters had been made quite comfortable. Gus was ushered into a wide hall where the floor was decorated with a swirling pattern of white sand. Every day a servant swept away the old sand and replaced it.

Voices could be heard coming from the next room.

"It's treason, gentlemen! Treason, I tell you."

That was the governor, Gus realized. He had heard him give a speech once. The governor's voice always rose when he got excited.

"Quite right, Your Excellency," said someone else.

Gus heard the murmured sounds of the servant speaking.

"Very well," said the governor. "Send him in."

The air in the dining room was heavy with the smell of rum punch. It was the food, though, that caught Gus's eye.

This was a meal Gus had seen only in his dreams. There were soup and fish, duck and goose. A great slab of beef sat by each gentleman. On the sideboard were beautiful jellies and pumpkin pies.

The governor was sitting at the head of the table. His two guests, Judge De Lancey and Squire Wilson, sat on either side. All three men had large napkins tied around their necks.

"Look at this rubbish!" sputtered the governor, squinting at his newspaper. He read aloud:

The people of New York think, as matters now stand, that their liberties and properties are precarious, and that slavery is likely to be entailed on them and their posterity, if some past things be not amended.

"Did you ever hear such a thing?" said the squire.

"Preposterous!" said De Lancey.

"You should arrest Zenger, Your Excellency,"

said the squire. "Send a message to all the rabble-rousers."

The governor smiled broadly. "Quite right, Squire, quite right." He turned to Gus. "So, you've brought me something from Bradford? Let's have it!"

Gus showed him the notice.

The governor read it carefully. "Yes, yes, this will do nicely." He took a bite of his food, stabbing at it with a piece of metal. At first Gus thought this was a knife, but a second look changed his mind.

"What are you staring at, boy?"

"Me, Your Excellency? I—I wasn't—"

"Come, come, I know a stare when I see one. Or are you calling me a liar?"

Gus swallowed nervously. Call the governor a liar? He had never meant any such thing. He had hoped, in fact, to say something showing his loyalty. Now he was too flustered to think clearly. "N-No, Your Excellency," he sputtered. "You are certainly no liar."

The governor laughed harshly. "I'm glad we're agreed on that point. So, tell me, what were you staring at?"

"I guess, maybe, the metal in your hand."

"This?" The governor held the silver utensil in the air. "It's called a fork, boy. It's all the rage in Europe."

"What's it for, Your Excellency?"

"To eat with, you dolt! At least for civilized folk."

The governor bellowed out an order. A few moments later a servant brought him some white paper, a brass inkwell, three freshly cut goosequill pens, and a silver shaker of sand.

Governor Cosby dipped the quill in the inkwell and scribbled a message. When he was done, he sprinkled the sand on the paper, blotting up the extra ink. Then he folded the letter and closed it with sealing wax.

He handed the letter to his servant and indicated it should be given to Gus.

"There, boy. I've written a message to your master. I trust you can deliver it quickly. Am I right?"

"Yes, Your Excellency."

"Then, go," said the governor. "Go!"

Gus went.

☞ SIX

Gus had to get up at dawn, but he often rose even earlier. A bookbinder on Duke Street sometimes lent Gus books that were for sale in his shop. The books could only be kept overnight, though. They had to be returned before the shop opened for business the next day.

Gus was a quick reader, but time for reading meant less time for sleep. And reading by candlelight sometimes put a strain on his eyes. Some books, like *Robinson Crusoe*, he had borrowed more than once to finish.

This morning, the eighteenth of November,

he dressed in the darkness of the Bradfords' attic and quietly descended the stairs. Under his arm was a handsome leather-bound edition of *Gulliver's Travels*. Gus had liked the first part about the Lilliputians. The rest had made his head ache.

The streets were quiet at this hour. He found the bookbinder's daughter, Anne, waiting in the shop.

"You're late," she whispered.

"Am I?" said Gus. There was a hint of sun on the eastern horizon.

"Well, maybe not," Anne admitted. Sometimes she lost her temper with Gus. It angered her that he could work as an apprentice and she could not. Oh, her father let her help out sometimes, but only when it didn't interfere with cooking and cleaning and making clothes.

Gus grinned at her. He knew what she was thinking, but there was nothing he could do about the ways of the world.

He took a moment to gaze at the many books around the shop. There were twenty or thirty of them, more than he had ever seen anywhere else.

"I wish I could own books," he said. "Imagine being able to just sit down and read whenever you wanted."

"Down in Philadelphia," said Anne, "they've started something for people who don't own books. It's called a social library."

"A library?" said Gus.

"It's a place where people go to borrow books. Not just anyone can go there, mind you, you have to be a member. And that costs money. But not as much as buying all the books yourself."

Gus just shook his head. Borrowing books whenever he wanted. Maybe New York would get a library soon.

"Will you be back tonight for another book?" Anne asked.

Gus yawned. "I'm afraid not. Yesterday I helped get paper from the mill in Elizabethtown. Today we'll be printing until late."

"Speaking of printing, did you hear the news?"

"What news?"

"Peter Zenger was arrested yesterday. The warrant for the arrest came from the governor himself. The sheriff took him off to jail."

Gus was glad. Zenger had been making trou-

ble for months. Now he would be brought to justice.

"I would like to hear more," said Gus, "but I should be getting back. Goodbye, Anne, and thank your father for me."

Gus returned to the Bradfords' in time for breakfast. Master Bradford often ate in silence, and expected his apprentice to do the same. Gus was hoping the master might make some comment about Zenger, but he didn't.

And then it was time to print the *Gazette*. Two people worked together in the effort. The sheets of paper were placed on the tympan one at a time. Then the carriage was run in and out. Afterward, the freshly inked paper was removed. A skilled team could print 240 pages—a token—in an hour. Gus's best was 180 pages—and sometimes he wrinkled the paper or blotted the ink.

Gus had not set the type this week, so he had not yet seen the news. As the day passed, he had a few moments to study the drying pages. Surprisingly, there was no mention of Zenger's arrest.

He later asked Master Bradford for an explanation.

"I will not allow that rascal to take up space in my newspaper," the master explained. "No doubt his own newspaper will carry a complete report."

"Will he keep publishing, then?" Gus asked.

Master Bradford shook his head. "A high bail has been set, but I know Peter Zenger. I only wish bail would muzzle him. He is a stubborn man. He will keep publishing, even if he has to do it from jail."

The printer wagged a finger at Gus. "A stubborn man can make friends. A stubborn and critical man makes mostly enemies."

Gus understood that. Zenger had criticized Governor Cosby, the chosen representative of the king. *Seditious libel*, it was called, a very serious charge. No person was allowed to speak ill of the government. If that was permitted, before long people might lose faith in the government itself. Therefore Zenger must be punished. Gus wouldn't have traded places with him for anything in the world.

☞ SEVEN

That winter was a harsh one. There was little snow, but the temperature often fell below freezing. Many mornings Gus broke the ice in a bucket of water before washing his face.

Master Bradford had turned out to be right about Peter Zenger. He was as stubborn as the cold weather, and neither showed any sign of breaking. His newspaper had missed one issue, but the explanation for that appeared in the next.

Gus did not usually read the *Weekly Journal*, but he did see it that week. Zenger wrote from prison that at first:

I was put under such Restraint that I had not the Liberty of Pen, Ink, or Paper, or to see, or speak with People.

That situation changed in a few days. However, Zenger's bail was set too high—£800—for him to afford it. So he stayed in jail, waiting for his trial. He continued to edit his newspaper, though, which his wife, Catherine, and his son, John, were still printing.

Two months passed with no change in the situation. Zenger's lawyers had questioned the judges' right to make a case against him, but they were not making much progress.

One thing that continued to surprise Gus was how little about Zenger's case ever appeared in the *Gazette*. Even if Zenger deserved imprisonment, his case was still news. The fact that Zenger continued to publish from jail only added interest to his situation. Yet aside from a note in December that accused Zenger of publishing "pieces tending to set the province in a flame, and to raise seditions and tumults," the *Gazette* ignored him.

This was something Zach reminded Gus of

one Sunday afternoon at the Collect Pond. Each boy had a pair of skates thrown over one shoulder.

"I thought the *Gazette* prided itself on reporting all the news," Zach was saying.

"I thought so, too," said Gus. "But Master Bradford treats Zenger as a special case."

Zach nodded. "I knew it was not your doing. But it is maddening all the same."

At the pond's edge, they sat down to put on their skates.

"I'm glad you were able to come today," said Gus. "This is the first free Sunday you've had in some time."

Zach hesitated. "I have been busy. There were meetings . . ."

Gus looked at him sharply. "Meetings? About what?"

Other people were sitting nearby, and Zach was wary of saying too much.

"Let's skate," he said abruptly.

The ice seemed a little mushy near the edge. The center of the pond, though, was smooth and hard.

"You have something to tell me?" said Gus.

"Only in confidence," Zach answered. "You understand that."

Gus nodded.

"I have been meeting with the Morrisites," said Zach.

"Oh," said Gus. The Morrisites were a group of prominent landowners and politicians who disliked the governor. They were headed by Lewis Morris, one of the wealthiest men in the colony. These were the men who had helped Peter Zenger start his newspaper.

"You'd best be careful," said Gus. "You could end up in jail, too. Peter Zenger clearly broke the law. Don't forget, the governor represents the king here in New York. And the king rules us all."

"Aye, so he does," said Zach. "But you have to admit he rules from a distance. I doubt we disturb good King George's thoughts very often."

Gus had never considered being in a king's thoughts at all. He pulled up short on his skates.

"Well, we're in the governor's thoughts, and those thoughts have not been pleasant of late."

Zach was not impressed. "The governor has

brought disfavor on himself," he said. "If he is not challenged, who knows what actions he will take?"

"Still, I caution you," said Gus. "Master Bradford speaks ill of such behavior. The authorities should not be challenged, he says."

Zach laughed. "Then he has a short memory. Why, your own master once challenged the authorities himself."

"What? When?"

"It was before he came to New York," Zach explained. "When Master Bradford first came to America forty years ago, he was a printer in Philadelphia. One time he printed a tract the Quaker government didn't like. He was arrested and his equipment was confiscated."

Gus was shocked. "What happened next?" he asked.

"Well, the equipment was returned some months later, but your master didn't forget. A few years later, the New York Council offered him the position of public printer. They needed someone to print their records and publish official documents. He took the job, and has stayed here ever since."

"Why have you not told me this before?" asked Gus.

"I only just learned it myself. Perhaps it explains why your master is so cautious now. Caution sits heavily on older shoulders. That is why they so often are stooped."

"Poor Richard?" said Gus.

Zach smiled. "No," he said, "I just made it up. I—Look out there!"

Gus dodged left as two younger children raced by. They sped across the ice, laughing in a game of tag.

Suddenly there was a large splash—and one child disappeared from view.

"Come on!" shouted Zach. "Quick!"

The other child had stopped and turned.

"Help!" he cried.

A moment later, the first child surfaced in the icy water. He thrashed around helplessly.

"Watch out," said Gus. "I think he fell in an old ice-fishing hole."

Zach skated close to the struggling boy.

"Hold on!" he said. "We're coming." He turned to Gus. "We'll make a chain."

Gus nodded.

Zach knelt down and lay spread-eagled on the ice. He didn't want the ice around the hole to break any further. Behind him Gus was spread-eagled, too. He was keeping a tight hold on Zach's ankles.

Slowly Zach wriggled forward, extending a hand to the frightened boy.

"Just a little farther. That's it. . . . That's it."

The ice beneath him cracked a little. The boy's fall had weakened it. The water crept toward him, seeping into his coat.

The panicky boy lunged for Zach. The freezing water splashed up and stung Zach's face. He blinked away tears.

"One moment! Stay calm! Grab my arms and kick. That's it. Now pull, Gus!"

Gus pulled for all he was worth.

☞ EIGHT

"How long before you'll get up, Lazybones?" asked Gus.

Zach smiled weakly from his bed. "I wish I knew," he sighed. "Poor Richard says, 'Early to bed and early to rise, makes a man healthy, wealthy, and wise.' At this rate, I will soon have the riches and wisdom of Solomon."

It had been seven days since the incident at the Collect Pond—the longest week of Gus's life. He had escaped unharmed, but Zach had caught a chill saving the young boy. Before another day had passed, he had collapsed on the floor of his master's office. For five days he had been feverish. Only now was he slowly mending.

As far as Gus was concerned, Zach was a hero. Oh, Gus knew *he* had helped, too, but Zach had been the decisive one. It reminded him of when Zach had saved him from the bullying boys. Zach never hesitated once he made a decision. He always plunged right in.

"What does the doctor say?" Gus asked.

Zach made a face. "He considered putting leeches on me—to draw out the sickness, he said. I didn't fancy that, so I decided to get better."

"Well, if you need anything, you let me know."

"I do have something to ask you," said Zach. He took a slow breath. "First, I should explain. A message has just arrived that must be delivered tonight."

"A message?" said Gus. "For whom?"

"William Smith."

Gus stiffened. William Smith was one of Peter Zenger's lawyers.

"My master fears to deliver it himself," Zach

explained. "The sheriff is watching his movements. I was to be the messenger. Nobody pays any mind to a lowly apprentice."

He stopped as a fit of coughing racked him.

"I was hoping yet to go," Zach continued. "But I can barely stand. So, I need your help."

Gus hesitated. "You know my feelings in this matter."

Zach sighed. "I thought perhaps they had changed. Last week when we were talking on the ice . . ."

"I know," said Gus. It was true that his feelings were less settled than before. More and more greedy stories had surfaced lately about the governor.

"It is nothing illegal I ask," said Zach. "Only to say, 'The fox lingers in the henhouse.'"

Gus sighed. Master Bradford would not approve. Still, Gus could not forget how Zach had always stood by him.

"You will be safe," said Zach. "I promise."

"As safe as Captain Kidd?" Gus asked, rubbing his neck.

"Safer than that, I hope. And remember what Poor Richard says—"

"Never mind," said Gus. "I'll do it, if only to keep Poor Richard happy."

The King's Arms was almost always a busy place. This night was no different. Local merchants and tradesmen mingled easily, sharing drinks and conversation by the flickering lanterns.

Gus had come as quickly as he could after supper. The message felt like hot lead inside him. He was anxious to be rid of it.

A smoky haze filled the tavern's meeting room. Gus approached the tavern-keeper, who was busy making flip. This drink was made from rum and beer and a little sugar. It was heated and stirred with a loggerhead, a red-hot poker.

"Have you seen William Smith?" Gus asked.

"Not tonight, boy. But his friends are sitting at a table against the wall." The tavern-keeper jerked his head toward the left. "No doubt he'll be along to join them."

Gus looked left. There at a table were James Alexander, Geradus Stuyvesant, and Cadwallader Colden. Alexander he knew already. Stuyvesant was a relative of a famous former Dutch governor of the city. The older man, Colden, was an author and scientist.

Gus was not sure what to do. Alexander and Smith were friends—they were defending Zenger together—but Zach had said nothing about giving the message to anyone else. It was probably safer to wait. Huddling in his cloak, Gus sat down on a bench and watched.

And then he noticed he was not the only one watching. Squire Wilson was sipping a pint of ale in a darkened corner. His face sagged peacefully, but his eyes glittered. Clearly it was not ale alone he was drinking in.

"Zenger's spirits are still good," James Alexander was saying. "Five months in jail have not quenched his spirit."

"And he'll be there five more, if I'm any judge," said Geradus Stuyvesant. "Our legal system crawls at a snail's pace. How goes that battle?"

Alexander sighed. "As you know, we have challenged the authority of the judges Cosby has appointed to oversee the case. He responds by creating new courts to suit his fancy. I believe we will outwit him yet."

Cadwallader Colden tapped his long clay pipe against his cheek. "Gentlemen," he said, "do not make the mistake of underestimating the governor. He may be a vain and blustery man, but beware! A fool can be more dangerous to those around him than he is to himself."

"A point well taken," said Alexander. "Ah, here comes our friend Smith."

A man had just entered, rubbing his hands together for warmth. Gus chewed his lip. How could he now deliver the message? What if the squire recognized him?

Raised voices in the middle of the room suddenly drew everyone's attention. Two farmers there were facing each other warily.

"I say the governor's a good man."

"Aye. Good at looking out for his own interests." The farmer picked up a loggerhead and thrust it in the air.

All eyes followed the two men, even Squire Wilson's.

Gus blinked. This is my chance, he thought. He rose, and pretended to stumble as he passed William Smith.

The lawyer reached out an arm to steady him.

"The fox lingers in the henhouse," hissed Gus.

Smith grinned at him. "He does, eh? Well, thank you, boy. And be careful to watch your step in future."

"That's just the drink talking," one of the farmers snorted.

"Well, if it is," said the other, "it knows what it's talking about."

"Oh, really?" His opponent picked up a poker of his own. The two were now at loggerheads.

It looked as if a fight might follow. Gus was naturally curious, but with his errand done, he was eager to be gone.

Mumbling a farewell to William Smith, he darted out the tavern door.

☞ NINE

Looking back, Gus admitted that the whole thing had been a little exciting. Still, that didn't keep him from feeling guilty. For days afterward he reddened whenever Master Bradford looked at him. Fortunately, his master did not notice these unseasonable flushes.

As days and then weeks passed, the fear of discovery gradually faded. The shop was busy, and his duties were many.

One morning in early May, Gus was setting type for the *Gazette*. He had already read the handwritten articles for this week's issue. Once again Gus was surprised at the news left out of the paper.

This news concerned Peter Zenger. On April 18th the governor's ally, Chief Justice De Lancey, had arranged matters so that James Alexander and William Smith could no longer defend Zenger in court. He had disbarred them. And replacing the two lawyers would be no easy task. There were not so many lawyers in New York, and even fewer who supported Zenger.

None of this, however, had been mentioned in the *Gazette*. When the first week passed with no word of the news, Gus had assumed that the article was still being written. By now it was clear that Master Bradford intended to ignore the incident.

This did not seem right to Gus. This disbarment was news, no matter what side he was on. How could Master Bradford just ignore it? This suggested that the governor and his allies weren't proud of their actions, and wished to keep them quiet.

Gus didn't like that.

And the disbarment did not seem right, either. Whatever Zenger's crime, he should be allowed to choose his own defenders. Was the governor's case so weak that he must bully his foes? Were these the actions of an honest man?

A sigh from Master Bradford drew his attention.

"This won't do," said the printer, inspecting a handbill. "This won't do at all."

Lately, the master had often complained about the quality of the printing. The problem lay in the type, which was clearly worn out.

Master Bradford stood up and stretched. "I thought we could manage till September, when the new type I've ordered will come from London." He drummed his fingers on the table. "I fear we cannot wait till then."

"Master Bradford?" said Gus.

"Yes?"

"Perhaps you could find some help in Philadelphia?"

The master brightened at that. His son Andrew was a successful printer in Philadelphia. Quite possibly he would have some type to spare.

"You may be right, Gus. And I have not seen Andrew and his family in some time. However, it is a hundred miles from here to Philadelphia. That is a journey of several days. And I am not as young as I once was." He smiled. "Since it was your idea, I believe I will take you with me."

"Me? To Philadelphia?"

"We'll go on Wednesday."

Gus could hardly believe it. He had not been out of New York since his family had arrived there. Going to Philadelphia seemed as likely as going to the moon.

Later that day he again delivered his newspapers. He dropped one off at Zach's office.

"You look fit to burst about something," said Zach.

Gus smiled. "It shows that much?"

"Yes, yes, it shows. So, tell me, what's the news?"

"Master Bradford is taking me to Philadelphia."

"But that's perfect," said Zach.

"I know. Imagine . . ." Gus stopped. Zach had this strange expression on his face. "Why do you think it's *perfect*?"

Zach coughed. "Well, it's a stroke of luck. You see, there was a meeting last night. Certain issues were raised." He paused. "Do I have your word this will pass no further?"

Gus nodded.

"As you know, James Alexander and William Smith can no longer defend Zenger in court. Lewis Morris and the others feel that if they appoint someone else from here, Chief Justice De Lancey will simply disbar him, too. Someone will be appointed to defend Zenger, but not someone who really believes in his cause. We need a lawyer from outside the city, someone to surprise and confuse them at the trial. Have you ever heard of Andrew Hamilton?"

"No."

"He's a lawyer in Philadelphia. He's old, in his eighties, even older than Master Bradford. But he's famous for his wit and wisdom. We want him to defend Zenger. And the sooner we act, the better. We need a courier to carry a letter, someone who will attract no attention. Could you do it?"

Gus didn't know what to say.

"This is important, Gus," said Zach. "No matter what you think of Zenger, surely he is entitled to a fair defense."

Gus agreed with that. But could he keep such a letter safe? What if it was discovered? This was far more than carrying a message to the King's Arms.

Unfortunately, Gus had no more time now to discuss the matter. His other deliveries were waiting. "I'll think on it," he said.

"Fair enough," said Zach. "We'll talk again to-morrow."

When Gus arrived at the Van Winkles' house, his mother was busy with the kitchen oven. It was baking day. Already she had burned a hot fire until the bricks glowed with the heat. Now she was sweeping out the wood and ashes.

"Good day to you, Augustus," said his mother. "Please take off your shoes. I'll not have you muddying the floor. I just washed it."

While Gus did as she asked, his mother filled the oven with pots of beans, three loaves of brown bread, and two pies. She pushed them in with a peel, a kind of shovel with a long handle.

"So," she said, closing the iron door, "you carry a burden today?"

"How can you tell?"

His mother smiled. "I could be mysterious, and just say a mother knows these things. But you keep twirling your fingers in your hair. It is your habit when you are troubled."

Gus told her about Zach and the letter.

Mistress Croft sighed. "The Van Winkles talk much of these things. It seems the governor grows bolder with each passing day."

Like a fox lingering in the henhouse, thought Gus.

It was so confusing. He could see Master Bradford's side of the matter. But he understood Zach's viewpoint, too. For a long time Gus's ideas had been neat and orderly, like rows of type set up to print. But now his ideas were all mixed up like pie—printer's pie.

"I wish I had never mentioned Philadelphia," he muttered.

"Remember," said his mother, "someone will carry the letter in any event. Life would be easy if there were always another person to take all the risks."

Gus sighed. "Master Bradford would not approve."

"And you want his approval?"

"Well, yes. He is a fine man."

"True," said his mother. "But he is also a man with a new wife and stepchildren. Master Bradford needs the governor's business, so he follows the governor's lead. That may be right for him. It need not be right for you. You are his apprentice, but that is in matters of business. It would be wrong, for example, to use his equipment or supplies against his wishes. In other matters, though, you should keep your own counsel."

"Then you think I should carry the message?"

She smiled. "I think the decision is yours."

Gus hesitated. "Should I not be loyal to my master?"

His mother shrugged. "Who knows what your master thinks, deep in his heart? He too was rebellious once." She sighed. "But he was younger then. You, however, are young now. And you will not be an apprentice forever."

"What if I am found out?"

"We will deal with that if it comes. But better to face that loss than to face fear and disappointment in your thoughts."

Gus took a deep breath. It was time for him to do something he believed in. The printer's pie in his mind had sorted itself out.

"Very well," he said, "I'll do it."

☞ TEN

The seats of the Philadelphia-bound passenger coach were not very comfortable. Gus didn't mind, though. An adventure wasn't supposed to have comfortable seats.

So far, he and Master Bradford were the only ones on board. Gus leaned left to look out the window. Then he winced. The edge of Zach's letter, which he had hidden under his shirt, was poking him in the stomach.

"Are you in pain, Gus?" Master Bradford asked.

"Just a bit of indigestion," said Gus.

"Too much pudding, I expect."

Gus blushed.

"Open up there!" commanded a voice from outside.

Gus reached over to undo the latch.

The door swung open and Squire Wilson climbed inside. Dust from his wig settled around the coach.

"So, Bradford, you too are traveling today."

"Yes. I go to visit my son in Philadelphia."

"I have business there as well," said the squire. "And the boy . . ."

"This is my apprentice, Augustus Croft."

The squire cast a hard glance at Gus.

"I have seen you in the shop." He frowned. "And around town, I believe."

Gus swallowed hard. Did he mean the tavern?

"You surprise me, Squire," said Master Bradford. "I would have thought the journey by sea would be faster and more to your liking."

Squire Wilson cleared his throat. "Sea voyages do not agree with me," he said.

Master Bradford nodded. "I suffer from the same complaint. Yet I fear this trip will have also its ups and downs."

76

He turned out to be right. The journey to Philadelphia was very bumpy. In some places the road was twelve feet across. In others it was little more than a wide path. Deep ruts and tree stumps littered the way. The coach made its way slowly over them all. Gus thought his teeth might fall out, they rattled around so much.

The best part of the journey was the stories Master Bradford told each evening after supper. At Gus's prodding, he explained how he had first come to Philadelphia as a young man in 1685.

"Lord Penn himself had arrived only four years earlier. The city was still being laid out then. I worked hard and brought over my wife, Elizabeth, in a few years. Things went well at first, but not everything turned out as I planned."

Gus knew about his master's old troubles, but he said nothing.

Master Bradford looked into the fire. "My son Andrew had better luck later on. He's done well, Andrew has, even with young Franklin nipping at his heels. You've heard of him, Gus?"

Gus nodded.

"Twelve years ago Ben Franklin came to me looking for work," Master Bradford recalled. "I had no openings at the time. I sent him to Andrew in Philadelphia. He gave him one or two jobs, I believe. Got him started."

When they arrived in Philadelphia, Gus was struck by how elegant the city was. Three-story brick buildings lined the streets, set off by lush green lawns and flowers already in bloom.

The coach let them off near the docks. Gus noticed a number of people dressed more plainly than the others. These were Quakers, Master Bradford explained. Quakers made up an important part of Pennsylvania's population, and they did not believe in wearing showy clothes.

Gus and Master Bradford soon came to Andrew Bradford's printing shop, just off one of the main squares. The greasy smell of ink filled the air as they entered.

Andrew was standing at one of the presses. He looked up as the door opened.

"Father! What a nice surprise!"

They greeted each other warmly. There was a small office in the back of the shop, and they retreated there for a few minutes. Gus amused himself meanwhile, watching others do the work he was used to doing himself.

A journeyman had just finished rubbing an inked leather sack across the letters in a form. Now he put a sheet of paper over the type and pressed down on it with a board. Removing the paper, he then examined the broadside for mistakes. Finding none, he was ready to run the press.

Master Bradford emerged from the office and called to Gus.

"I have an errand for you at a bookseller's on Walnut Street. Don't get lost, and be back for supper."

Gus nodded. If he was quick about it, he could probably find time to deliver his letter. According to his map, Walnut Street was close to Andrew Hamilton's office. He might not get a better chance.

Philadelphia was bigger than New York, and laid out more neatly. The streets were filled with carriages. There were even a few sedan chairs, in which wealthy people sat while servants carried them about.

"You there, boy!"

Gus turned around and found himself facing Squire Wilson. The squire was holding a map of Philadelphia. The map was upside down.

"Croft, isn't it? I seem to have lost my way. I suppose you're on an errand for your master?"

"Well, yes, and—"

"It will have to wait. I have several purchases to make, and I will need someone to carry them back to my lodgings. You will do nicely."

"But I—"

"Come, come, boy. We're wasting time."

Glumly, Gus followed the squire down Market Street. He was very aware of the letter pressing against his stomach. Andrew Hamilton's office was so close, but what did that matter now? The squire was likely to keep Gus busy until his free time was gone.

"Do you smell something burning?"

The squire had stopped. As he stood there, glancing up the street, smoke began pouring out the window of a town house.

Squire Wilson sniffed the air. "Kitchen fire, I think."

"Move aside there!"

Gus jumped to the side as men rushed by pulling a fire engine. It was much like one Gus had seen in New York, with pumping handles and foot treadles. Gus hoped the firemen were more skilled here than they were at home. In New York the first house the new engines tried to protect had burned to the ground.

As the men rushed by, a loose hose snagged Gus's foot. He tumbled to his knees.

The letter fell out of his shirt.

"Sorry, there! Stay clear!"

Gus dove to retrieve the letter, but as he did, the squire spotted it as well.

"Here now, boy, what's that?"

"Just a letter, Squire. Nothing to trouble—"

"It looks official. Let me see—*Aagggh!*"

A cold stream of water had doused the squire's back. He turned around—and another stream hit his face, knocking off his wig and hat.

"Hold that hose tighter!" shouted the fireman. "Aim it at the window."

The squire stood there, dripping wet, his face turning a purple hue. The letter was forgotten, his packages were forgotten, everything was forgotten as the squire lost his temper.

"This outrage will not be tolerated! Do you know who I am?"

"You're someone who should stand clear, sir," said the leader of the fire brigade. "Otherwise you may get wet again."

"You haven't heard the last of this," the squire raged.

The gathering crowd had begun to laugh, and the squire was now aware of them. His anger gave way to embarrassment.

"Shall we continue with your errands?" Gus asked, trying hard to keep a straight face.

"Hang the packages! I must get changed. And just look at this wig." He squeezed some water out of it. "Oh, bother! You'd better go on about your master's business."

And having said that, he stalked off.

Gus darted the other way, in case the squire had a sudden change of heart. Then he consulted his map, and walked quickly to Andrew Hamilton's office.

As he entered, he came upon an older man examining a lengthy document.

"Excuse me, sir, I'm looking for Andrew Hamilton."

"Then I would say you have found him."

"I bring you a letter, sir. From New York."

Gus handed it over.

"Come inside," said the lawyer, indicating the next room. "It is a better place to think, and certainly a better one to sit."

He led Gus into a handsome office filled with fine wood furniture. Gus felt a little uncomfortable in his stained clothes. Andrew Hamilton, though, did not seem troubled by them. He motioned Gus to a comfortable chair.

The lawyer sat down too, and took a few minutes to read the letter.

"Your friends are facing an interesting problem," he said finally. "Governor Cosby, whatever his legal rights, seems to be riding roughshod over common sense."

Gus nodded. He had not been able to put it into words before, but that was how he thought of it, too.

"It's a pity common sense is such a rare commodity," said Hamilton. "After all, Zenger is only printing the truth. Should a man be punished for that? Why, if printing the truth is criminal, then lies and deceit will always hold the upper hand."

Hamilton's clerk appeared in the doorway, heralding the arrival of the lawyer's next appointment.

"Very well," he said, rising.

Gus rose, too.

"The letter asks for no immediate reply, and perhaps it would be better to put nothing in writing at this time. But you may tell your friends, I will be ready when they need me."

"Thank you," said Gus. Then he took his leave.

Gus saw little more of Philadelphia during his stay. Master Bradford kept him busy assembling the font of type he needed from Andrew's supplies. Gus also helped to cast a few extra letters to complete the set.

On the long ride back to New York, Gus thought how disappointed Zach would be when he got back. Oh, he would be glad that Gus had delivered the letter safely and that Andrew Hamilton had agreed to help Peter Zenger. But Zach had also been hoping that Gus would be able to meet Richard Saunders. However, there hadn't been time. Master Bradford took no chance of overstaying his welcome, even with his own son. As Poor Richard himself would say, "Fish and visitors stink in three days."

☞ ELEVEN

The summer of 1735 was hot and humid in New York. One Sunday in late July, Gus and Zach went swimming in the Collect Pond. It was hard to believe this was the same place where the boy had fallen through the ice.

"No skating today," said a voice behind them.

It was Anne. She had come to the pond with her parents.

The three children walked along the pond's edge, skipping stones in the water.

"I heard my parents talking this morning,"

said Anne. "The Zenger trial is set to begin next month."

Gus and Zach nodded.

Anne was not hopeful about it. "I've read about the libel laws," she said. "If nothing is changed, Zenger really must be found guilty." She sighed. She was as much on Zenger's side as Zach.

"But perhaps something will be changed," said Zach. "The judge is against Zenger, that we know. Our hope lies with the jury. They will make the final decision."

The twelve-man jury had been chosen that month from the list of New York freeholders. These were all men who owned land in the colony, and therefore were allowed to participate in such matters.

Gus skimmed a stone over the water. "Can the jury really do anything it wants?"

Zach nodded.

"Well, then," said Gus, "I hope everyone is paying attention."

Zenger's trial took place on Monday, August 4th. Master Bradford did not see it as a special day, and his schedule remained unchanged. As usual, Gus spent his time delivering the *Gazette* to subscribers around town. His route took him past the courthouse, though, and he couldn't resist stopping for a look.

The courtroom itself was jammed with people, and Gus had no chance of entering. But on such a hot day all the windows were open. He managed to get close enough to see and hear what was going on.

The participants all looked very serious in their white powdered wigs and long robes. As Gus watched, the attorney general, Richard Bradley, finished presenting the government's case. The matter was a simple one, he argued. The chief justice had already determined that the governor had been libeled in the *New-York Weekly Journal.* That was against the law. If the jury determined that Zenger was responsible for this libel, then he was guilty as charged.

The attorney general surveyed the courtroom confidently. With Zenger's best defenders barred from speaking, he expected the case to be decided quickly.

Zenger's lawyer was John Chambers, appointed by the court after the disbarment of Alexander and Smith. His opening speech was short and lacking much energy. Like many others, he clearly felt there was little room to present this case.

At that point a distinguished-looking man rose from his seat. Gus recognized him at once.

"May it please Your Honor," said Andrew Hamilton, "I am concerned in this cause on the part of Mr. Zenger, the defendant."

The judge granted him permission to speak.

The lawyer's mellow voice drew everyone's attention. He was clearly at home in the courtroom. Gus was as curious as the rest about what Hamilton would say next.

The Philadelphia lawyer began by admitting that Zenger had both printed and published the two newspaper articles.

As far as Mr. Bradley was concerned, that ended the case, but Hamilton was not finished yet.

"I hope," he said, "it is not our bare printing and publishing a paper that will make it a libel. The words themselves must be libelous, that is false, scandalous, and seditious, or else we are not guilty."

This was a new argument, one that made people think. But Hamilton was not done yet. His main point was that it was the jury, not the judge, who should decide whether libel had taken place.

Current English laws, said Hamilton, were not made with colonial governors in mind. What kind of laws would protect governors from the consequences of their own misdeeds? Surely not a just law.

There was a murmur in the courtroom. Many colonists had begun to resent the interference from their mother country.

Gus knew that Hamilton had gained the crowd's sympathy. He hoped the jury was being swayed as well.

"The question before the court, and you, gentlemen of the jury, is not of small nor private concern; it is not the cause of a poor printer, nor of New York alone, which we are now trying. No! It may in its consequence affect every freeman who lives under a British government on the main of America. It is the best cause. It is the cause of liberty!"

Gus almost shouted out in agreement, but at the last moment he remembered where he was.

When both lawyers had finished, the jury withdrew to consider the case. Gus knew he should be going, but his curiosity was too great. What would the jury decide?

His patience was rewarded because the jury did not deliberate very long. They soon filed back in and took their seats.

The courtroom was hushed.

Chief Justice De Lancey asked the jury if it had reached a verdict.

"We have, Your Honor," said the jury foreman, Thomas Hunt. "We find the defendant, John Peter Zenger, not guilty."

 # TWELVE

"Not guilty."

The words echoed in Gus's mind as he stood in the churchyard listening to the minister speak. He had never forgotten the sense of rightness he had felt when the verdict was announced. It had been a lucky day for printers and for others as well.

Eleven years had passed since then. Now he was standing, with Zach and a few others, to pay his final respects to John Peter Zenger. The stubborn printer had died two days before, after several years of ill health. Gus had never been friends with Zenger, but he had always admired the veteran printer's gumption.

The service was soon ended.

Gus turned to see a bent figure standing a little way off. He had removed his hat and stood quietly among the trees.

It was Master Bradford. He was almost ninety now, and he leaned heavily upon his walking stick.

Gus walked over to his side. "It is good to see you, master."

Master Bradford put a friendly hand on Gus's shoulder. The hand shook.

"He was, after all, my apprentice, too," said the master, glancing back at the churchyard.

"So he was."

Gus saw Master Bradford home. They talked little on the way, but were glad of each other's company. The master had never learned about the small part Gus had played in Zenger's defense. It was just as well, thought Gus, who had continued to serve Master Bradford faithfully until his apprenticeship was up.

A short while later, Gus hurried back to his own shop. On the way he passed five buildings

under construction. New York was a bustling town in 1746. Gus had opened his shop only six months before, but he and his wife were hopeful about the future. Someday New York would be a great city, and they planned to be a part of it.

The bell on the door rang as he entered the shop. His wife looked up from one of the presses. She was experimenting with a new typeface, one she had designed herself.

"How did it go?" she asked.

"It was a proper burial," said Gus. "Decently attended. And Anne, you'll never guess who showed up! Master Bradford himself."

"So he had a weak spot for his former apprentice, after all."

"Aye. We printers have to stick together."

"What will happen to the Zengers now?" Anne asked.

"I've heard his wife and son will keep up the *Weekly Journal.*"

She smiled. "And you, no doubt, will keep up your subscription."

"Of course. It's important to keep an eye on your competition."

There was room in New York for more printers now. And, thankfully, none of them had to deal with Governor Cosby. He had died only two years after the trial. His successors, for the most part, had been a distinct improvement.

The opening of the shop door roused Gus from his thoughts. Two visitors, a man and a boy, had arrived. Gus was expecting them. The man was John Kingston, a sea captain. He was a cousin of Zach, whose law practice was established around the corner. The boy, Jamie, was Kingston's son. John Kingston had run away to sea at twelve, but Jamie had no wish to follow in his father's footsteps.

Jamie had shown a fondness for words, however. And so John Kingston had approached Gus about taking Jamie on as an apprentice.

Father and son stood before the young printer expectantly.

Gus cleared his throat, trying to sound more grown-up than he felt. "So, are you ready to begin your apprenticeship?"

"Yes, Master Croft."

Gus smiled. Jamie was sharp-eyed and curious, both useful traits for what lay ahead. He might not know much about the printing process yet.

But he would learn.

Afterword

The Printer's Apprentice is a fictional story surrounding the real arrest and trial of John Peter Zenger. This unassuming printer had no pretensions to greatness. He never imagined that his case would be remembered as a famous episode in early American history.

According to English law, no member of the government could be criticized in print. It didn't matter whether or not the official deserved the criticism. Under such a law Peter Zenger's arrest was certainly logical and his guilt seemed all but assured. Only Andrew Hamilton's appeal to the jury—to look beyond the law—saved the day.

While the main character, Augustus Croft, is fictional, his story dovetails into the actual events and customs of the era. The printing and papermaking processes Gus participates in were the methods used in colonial America. The facts of his apprenticeship are accurate as well. Serving with a master in a particular trade was a common path for boys of a certain age and background.

Although fact and fiction are thoroughly mingled in *The Printer's Apprentice,* the context is genuine. All the factual occurrences (for example, the time of Zenger's arrest and the months he spent in prison) have been incorporated into the story at the time and in the manner they actually happened.

Zenger himself, as well as William Bradford, his son Andrew, James Alexander, and Governor Cosby, were all real people. Their dialogue is invented, but each of them participated in the events of the period as portrayed here. Ironically, Zenger really was an apprentice of William Bradford in his younger years. As for Benjamin

Franklin, he did indeed come to William Bradford looking for work in 1723, and Bradford did send him on to his son in Philadelphia. Although his role in this book is secondary, William Bradford was a central figure in the early printing history of the colonies.

At the trial itself, Chief Justice De Lancey; Attorney General Richard Bradley; Zenger's appointed lawyer, John Chambers; and the Philadelphia lawyer Andrew Hamilton were all actual participants. (In fact, Hamilton's speech to the jury in Chapter Eleven was not invented for this story. His words are quoted from the written record of James Alexander, who masterminded Zenger's defense.)

John Peter Zenger never saw himself as a revolutionary figure. In many ways he was just doing his job. But he took that job seriously. His courtroom acquittal was an early sign that American colonists were unhappy with English rule. Most importantly, his actions as a printer and the results of his trial were not forgotten. His experience became a reference point for the idea of freedom of the press, an idea later incorporated into the American Bill of Rights.